The Soccer Monsters

By Jaden Sorkin

Illustrations by Deanna First

To my my dad Ian, the best coach

a kid could ask for and to

all my soccer friends over the years…

Have you ever heard of the story of the soccer monsters? You haven't? Well, Adam and David have.

Adam and David were the best of friends who loved playing soccer together.

Until one day...

both of their dads became their coaches...but for OPPOSITE teams.

Adam and David did not play together anymore. They had to practice every day.

Adam was playing for the Alien Beams...

While David played for the
Dynamite Dinos

David's father made sure that David practiced running as fast as he could and as much as he would.

While David's Dad made him dribble the ball up and down the field for hours.

Both teams were so good they
made it to the finals.

Their dads were very happy.

But Adam and David were not.
They did not want to play
against each other.

Both boys were sad…and missed just having FUN together.

But they did all they could to
win to make their dads glad.

The night before the final game,

David had terrible terrible NIGHTMARES…

Adam had the same awful dream...Soccer Monsters everywhere!

There were monsters on the soccer field! Very Scary Monsters!

RUN, PASS,

SCORE! The Monsters yelled.

Adam and David then realized in horror

that the monsters they feared…

were really their coaches all along!

Who were also their dads.

The scariest part of the dream was that David became a real DINO.

And Adam became a real Alien!

GAME DAY...

The next day, Adam and David both arrived for

the game and

they were both scared to play.

The dream and the monsters

felt so very very real.

It was time for Adam and David to talk to their Dads... They told them just how they both felt.

Their dads understood and told them that all they ever want is for them to be happy.

Adam and David were just
happy to have their
friendship back!

So they called off the final game and had a friendly match instead.

The Score didn't matter. All that mattered was they had FUN!

PLAY FOR FRIENDSHIP

Sports is a wonderful way to help form long lasting friendships that last a life time. It helps team work and leadership as well.

PLAY TO KEEP ACTIVE

Sports helps keep kids stay active and healthy.

It is great for getting outside in the fresh air.

PLAY FOR YOURSELF

Sports helps build

confidence and self-esteem

that lasts a lifetime!

Sports also helps kids

become leaders and work

hard.

Made in the USA
Columbia, SC
09 November 2020

24218315R00018